The Diamond in the Onion Suit

Mickey Michaels

ISBN-10: 0-9644761-6-9
ISBN-13: 978-0-9644761-6-5

1

Once upon a time, there was a little onion, born into a world of other onions, all of whom looked pretty much alike.

When she was born, she didn't have any layers of onion skin to protect her because she was, after all, only a baby onion. In fact, she was kind of bright and shiny and funny-looking. But that's how all baby onions look. All the grown-up onions knew she would grow her layers of onion skin soon enough.

At the time she was born, grown-up onions believed it would "spoil" a baby onion if you fed it and watered it whenever it cried. Onions had to be fed and watered on a strict schedule.

So the baby onion cried whenever she felt hungry, but no one came to feed her. Sometimes she was really, really hungry and cried and cried a lot. Sometimes she felt like she might starve to death! Of course, she wouldn't have starved because the grown-up onions knew when it was feeding time and always did come to feed her when it was the right time, according to the schedule.

The grown-up onions were doing this out of love, because they truly believed a proper feeding schedule was the very best way to make their precious baby onion grow up strong and healthy and not be "spoiled."

But the baby onion had no way of knowing this because she was, after all, only a baby. What she learned from this was that the world is a pretty tough place, and that she had better learn to take care of herself because she certainly couldn't count on anyone else to do it.

And the first layer of onion skin appeared.

After a while, the baby onion grew big enough to feed herself, so she didn't have to worry about starving anymore. And she also became very good at taking care of herself because, of course, she couldn't trust anyone else to do it.

This was a very useful skill, and it served her well throughout her life. In fact, a lot of onions admired her for it. Other onions seldom even tried to take care of her because it was so obvious that she could take care of herself. If one would occasionally try in some way to take care of her, she wouldn't even let him because she knew that all good onions are supposed to take care of themselves.

And over the years, this layer of onion skin grew heavy and tough.

2

For the first couple of years, life was good. The mother onion was always there to take care of her, but the best part of the day was when the father onion came home from work. He was so excited to see her, and he would talk to her and play with her, and she knew he really loved her. This was great!

But when she was two years old, something bad happened. The mother onion had another little baby onion, and this one was a boy onion! The mother onion still took good care of her, but now, when the father onion came home from work, he played with the baby boy onion! Of course, he didn't ignore the little girl onion, because he was a good father and a loving father. He loved both of them equally, but now he had two little onions and couldn't spend all of his time playing with his little girl onion like he had before.

But the little girl onion had no way of knowing this because she was, after all, only two years old. What she learned from this was that boy onions are better than girl onions, and because she was only a girl onion, she wasn't good enough.

And another layer of onion skin appeared.

As she grew older, the little girl onion did find a way to get the father onion to keep on playing with her, and that was to act like a boy onion. In fact, she became very good at this. She became very good at something called "onionball," which the father onion loved, so she always got to be with him whenever it was time to play onionball or go to a game. She got so good that the father onion almost never had to tell her, "You're throwing the ball like a *girl* onion!" She knew throwing like a *girl* onion meant you weren't good enough.

She got very good at many different kinds of onionball. She got so good that she knew more about them and could play them better than many of the boy onions. And she came to love onionball, and it gave her much pleasure throughout her life. Often, over years, boy onions and man onions would tell her they thought of her as "one of the boy onions," which she took to be a very high compliment.

And over the years, this layer of onion skin grew heavier and tougher.

3

Things went along pretty well for a while until the little girl onion got to be about five years old. This was when the mother and father onion told her it was time for her to go to onion school.

She wasn't sure she wanted to go to onion school—or anywhere else, for that matter. It felt pretty comfortable and safe just where she was, staying at home with the mother onion all day. She had even decided she liked playing with her little brother onion. He was okay after all, and they had fun playing. She was used to things just the way they were.

She had no idea what onion school would be like, or what she was supposed to do there, or whether it would be any fun at all. But the mother and father onions said she was getting to be a big little onion and all big little onions had to go to onion school to learn important things.

She didn't know why she needed to go to onion school. She already knew how to read, and she couldn't imagine what else there was to learn that could be of any use to her. She would much rather stay home with her mother and brother onion.

Why were they making her go away? Maybe they didn't want her around anymore. Going to onion school was scary, but if they didn't want her at home anymore, she'd better go to onion school like she was told.

Her first day at onion school was even worse than she had imagined. There were lots of little onions about her size, but she had no idea who they were or what she was supposed to do. They were all in a room called the 1B, which was for new little onions just starting onion school, and they all looked just as confused as she was. At the front of the room was a very large onion who looked very stern and called herself the "teachonion."

The teachonion told them the main thing they were going to learn in 1B was how to read. This was her chance! She already knew how to read! Once they found out she could read, maybe they would let her go home and play instead of having to be here at onion school!

So she said to the teachonion, "I already know how to read." The teachonion said, "We'll see about that," and took her out into the hall. From a large bag, the teachonion pulled out a book called *Fun with Dick and Jane Onion* and said, "Read this." *Fun with Dick and Jane Onion* was not a very interesting book, but it was easy to read, so the little girl onion started reading it out loud to the teachonion like she was told.

The teachonion got very excited and said, "Wait a minute." Then she called two other teachonions out into the hall and said, "Read some more." So the little girl onion read some more for all of them.

All the teachonions got very excited, and they talked among themselves for awhile. Finally one of the teachonions said, "Put her in the 1A." The little girl onion had no idea why everyone was making such a fuss. She wondered if she had done something wrong and was going to be punished. She wondered what it meant to be put in the 1A.

The teachonions took her down the hall to another room that was filled with different little onions with a different teachonion at the front of the room. They sat her at a little desk in the back of the room and said, "Here. You'll be in this room now."

The little girl onion looked all around her and tried to figure out what was going on. The little onions in this room didn't look much bigger than those in the 1B room, but there was one huge difference.

All these little onions seemed to already know each other and already know exactly what they were supposed to do at onion school. None of them paid any attention to her, and no one told her what she was supposed to do.

The little girl onion felt scared and confused and very sad. She would much rather be back at home, but she couldn't stay home anymore. She had to stay here with these new onions, but they didn't seem to want her around either.

Now, the teachonions had done what they knew was best for a little onion who already knew how to read. They skipped her a grade from the 1B to the 1A. But the little girl onion had no way of knowing this because, after all, she was only five years old and knew nothing at all about onion school and how it works.

What she learned from all this was: "I'm different, and I don't fit in. There's something wrong."

And another layer of onion skin appeared.

She knew she didn't fit in, but she also knew she had to make the best of it. She had to stay here at onion school, whether she liked it or not, so she'd better figure out what she needed to do.

She didn't want to call attention to herself. The last time she did that, they put her in the 1A, which was not a good thing. And she didn't want the other onions to know she didn't fit in. Then they would know she was different, and being different wasn't good. She just wanted to be like all the other onions.

Maybe if she was just quiet and did what she was told, nobody would notice her. Maybe if she just watched the other little onions and did whatever they did, she could be like them—or at least, look like them. Maybe if she could just keep up a good front, no one would know she didn't fit in.

So she tried this, and it seemed to work. She did whatever she was told and was very careful not to call attention to herself. And she did her best to look and act exactly like all the other onions.

And over the years, this layer of onion skin grew heavier and tougher.

4

A few more years went by, and the little girl onion grew bigger and stronger and taller— much taller. By the time she got to junior onion school, she was taller than almost all the boy onions.

This was okay until she began to look at the boy onions in a different kind of way. She noticed that the boy onions didn't seem interested in playing onionball with her anymore. Instead, they began to pair up with girl onions and do something they called "going together"—whatever that meant.

She even found that some of the girl onions she thought were her best onion friends didn't want to do things with her anymore because they were "going with" boy onions. It seemed that every onion who was any onion was "going with" another onion. And if she wasn't "going with" a boy onion, she simply didn't belong.

This feeling was familiar. It was just like the way she felt when she was five years old and first knew she didn't fit in. But this feeling made her even more uncomfortable now. All the junior onions were forming little groups and deciding who could belong, and it was terribly important to belong. Grown-up onions talked about "peer onions" and said it wasn't important to belong. But grown-up onions just didn't understand.

She wanted desperately to belong. She looked around and tried to figure out which onions belonged and which onions didn't. She discovered that almost all the girl onions who did belong were little, cute, and pretty onions. And the ones who were the littlest, cutest, and prettiest were something called "cheeronions."

Everyone thought they were the very best onions. They certainly thought so themselves, and she knew they must be right. All the boy onions wanted to "go with" a cheeronion. The cheeronions could "go with" any boy onion they wanted to, and the ones they did "go with" were the very best, most desirable boy onions: The captains and stars of the onionball teams!

If she could get to be a cheeronion, then she would be little, cute, and pretty. All the best boy onions would want to "go with" her, and she would belong. She had it figured out! This was the answer! She would become a cheeronion, and life would be great!

Now, getting to be a cheeronion was not easy. You couldn't just be one because you wanted to. There were a whole lot of onion tricks you had to learn how to do. You had to be able to do jumps, splits, flips, and onionwheels, all the while yelling, "Fight, Onions, Fight!" as loud as you could. Then you had to pass a test called a "tryout," where other onions would tell you if you were good enough and if you could belong.

She practiced and practiced doing all the onion tricks, even though for an onion as tall as she was, these tricks were very difficult. The day before the tryout, she wanted to show her mother onion the tricks she had been practicing. So she went into the house, where her mother was sitting in the onion room.

She was really excited about this one particular trick that she had gotten really good at. It started with some little jumps and a little yelling, and it ended with a BIG LEAP and a BIG YELL, leaping as high as she could and shoving her fist high in the air and yelling, "Fight, Onions, FIGHT!" As she yelled the last "FIGHT!" she leaped so high and shoved her fist so high into the air that her fist punched a hole right through the onion room ceiling! (This happened because she was so very tall, you see.)

At that moment, she *knew* that she was *not* little, cute, and pretty, that she would never be little, cute, and pretty, and it was absurd to think that she could ever be a cheeronion. She was big, clumsy, and awkward. She could never be a cheeronion, she could never "go with" a boy onion, and she could never belong.

And another layer of onion skin appeared.

5

So now what? If she could never belong, that meant no one would ever take care of her, so she had better get really good at taking care of herself. Of course, she had known this ever since she was a baby onion, but she hadn't really wanted to believe it. Now she knew it must be so.

How could she take care of herself? Maybe she could be smart! Her father onion was very smart, and he took care of himself and the whole onion family. But the father onion also worked very hard. So just being smart wasn't enough. You also had to be hard-working. You had to be smart *and* hard-working if you were ever going to be able to take care of yourself.

She didn't know if she could be smart, but she knew she could be hard-working. Maybe if she worked hard enough, she could also get smart.

She worked hard. She worked very, very hard. She got very, very good grades at onion school. (Grades are little letters they attach to you in onion school to tell if you are smart.)

The teachonions at onion school told her she was smart. The other student onions told her she was smart. In fact, once when one of the boy onions asked to see her onion card, he said, "Wow! If the onion school ever attached all those letters to me, my father would buy me an onionmobile!"

But her father never bought her an onionmobile. And he never told her she was smart. Whenever she showed him all the little letters that had been attached to her, he would just say, "That's nice," which made it clear to her that these letters were really not anything special, and they certainly didn't mean she was smart.

The father onion did this out of love, because he believed too much praise would "spoil" a little onion. But she had no way of knowing this because she was, after all, still a very young onion. So no matter what she did, she never thought of it as anything special and never gave herself any particular credit for doing it. She always figured that if she could do it, any onion could.

At times, this rather confused her. All the people at onion school were telling her she was smart. But her father onion didn't think she was smart. That's what made it confusing.

Then she figured it out! She knew her father was smarter than all the onions at onion school. And if he thought she wasn't smart, then he must be right. She *wasn't* smart, and any onion who thought she *was* smart must be STUPID!

There! That was it! She had it figured out!

She wasn't smart, but she *was* hard-working. And maybe if she worked hard enough, that could make up for not being smart, and she would still be able to take care of herself.

She continued to work very, very hard, and she continued to get lots and lots of those little letters attached to her. When her class left senior onion school, they had a big ceremony called graduonion. And she was something called Valedictonion and got something called a National Merit Onionship. Some onions thought all this was a big deal, but she knew it really didn't mean anything except that she was hard-working. But maybe that would be enough.

And another layer of onion skin appeared.

Being hard-working did serve her well. She went to the University of Onion (U of Onion), which was considered one of the finest in the country. They put her into a special program called Honors Onions, which was supposed to be only for onions who were smart. The other onions in this program really *were* smart, but for so many years she had been fooling onions into thinking she was smart when she was really only hard-working that she just went along with it. During one of her years at the U of Onion, they even gave her a special prize, which was supposed to go to the smartest onion. Boy, did she have them fooled!

And over the years, this layer of onion skin grew heavier and tougher.

6

While she was at the U of Onion, she noticed something that, for some reason, brought up certain feelings she had first noticed back in junior onion school.

By this time, she already knew about the little letters that onion schools attach to you to tell you if you are smart (which she now knew did not actually mean that at all). But at the University, they had another kind of letters—funny-looking letters that were not attached to you by the teachonions or the school, but by the other onions, and these letters told you if you could belong.

The onions who could belong got little letters attached to them, like "KKG" or "ADP." Only they didn't look like regular letters. Some of them looked like pyramids and some looked like little houses, and they had funny names. The onions who could belong got to live in sister onion houses. Mostly, the girl onions who could belong were little, cute, and pretty.

Those who lived in the sister onion houses attached other letters to the rest of the onions, whether they wanted them or not. The letters they attached were "GDI," which was considered a very funny joke and meant you didn't belong. The onions who didn't belong lived in the onion dorms.

She noticed something else about the little, cute, and pretty onions who lived in the sister onion houses. Many of them said they had come to the U of Onion to get a degree they called their "M.R.S." This meant they were going to catch a boy onion who would take care of them forever because these girl onions knew they certainly couldn't take care of themselves. The very best catch would be a boy onion who was going to make lots and lots of money, because that meant you would really, really be taken care of.

She found this all very interesting. But by now, she already knew that she would never be little, cute, and pretty, and that she would never belong. No one would ever take care of her, and she was going to have to take care of herself. Even though she wasn't really smart, she was really hardworking, and maybe that would be enough.

She remembered how much it had hurt when she had tried to be a cheeronion and had failed. She knew she didn't want to be hurt like that again. So what had she learned from her past? She knew the answer, and she knew what to do. Trying to belong would be much too risky, and it would hurt too much if she failed. It would be much safer to just pretend she didn't care.

So she didn't even try to join one of the sister onion houses. She already knew she could never belong. So she just pretended she didn't want to.

And another layer of onion skin appeared.

She tried not to think about belonging and just continued to work hard. And continuing to work hard served her well. When she left the U of Onion, the school attached a final group of letters to her at the big graduonion ceremony. These letters were B.A., M.A., and PBK (the last three letters meant you got very high grades). They were supposed to mean that you were smart *and* hard-working. But by now, she knew of course they really didn't mean that.

And the layers of onion skin grew heavier and tougher.

7

After graduonion, she went out to work, in order to become a "businessonion." This was a long time ago, and at that time, female onions were not supposed to be businessonions who had good jobs and earned lots of money. Only the male onions were supposed to be businessonions. They would earn the money and take care of the female onions, who were supposed to be "houseonions" and stay home and take care of the house and have baby onions.

This system seemed to work fine for some onions, but it seemed to her that it only worked if you were little, cute, and pretty, and you could "catch" a businessonion who was willing to take care of you. Of course, for her, this was impossible. She had to take care of herself.

But she really didn't mind. She thought being a businessonion was a lot more interesting than being a houseonion. In fact, it was really kind of fun. It was like playing onionball with her father and getting to be "one of the boy onions," which she knew was a great thing to be.

She worked hard, which she had already learned how to do, and it served her well. And she was very successful as a businessonion. In fact, she was a much better businessonion than most of the male onions. (In those days, you *had* to be better if you were a female onion because most onions believed male onions were much better and smarter than female onions, and male and female onions were not treated equally. But that was a long time ago, and of course, female onions don't have those kinds of problems today.)

She loved being a businessonion. And she made lots of money, so she was able to take very good care of herself. She didn't *need* a male onion to take care of her because she could do a much better job of it herself.

Even though she didn't *need* a male onion, she still really enjoyed being with them. Every now and then, she would even "go with" a male onion, like she used to see the other onions do, starting way back in junior onion school.

Sometimes a male onion would tell her she was pretty or smart, but she knew that was ridiculous. In fact, anyone who would even say things like that must be stupid. Whenever she found out a male onion was that stupid, she would decide to quit "going with" him.

One time a male onion she was "going with" told her he was crazy about her and wanted to marry her and take care of her! She realized at once that this onion was REALLY, REALLY STUPID—and she couldn't dump him fast enough!

And another layer of onion skin appeared.

Mostly she would "go with" male onions who didn't make a big fuss over her. This was what she was used to. They reminded her of her father. She thought they must be smart, like her father.

And over the years, the layers of onion skin grew heavier and tougher.

8

This went on for several years, and by now almost all her girl onion friends were marrying businessonions and becoming houseonions. Even though she loved being a businessonion, she thought she might be missing something. She began to wonder what it might be like to be a houseonion—to belong, to be taken care of.

At this time, she was "going with" a very nice male onion. He had "good character" and they had lots of "things in common." All sensible onions knew these were the qualities that made a successful union of onions.

She knew this nice male onion was not as super-smart and super-successful as her father, but then, no onion was. And she also realized something else. Whenever she was with other onions who were especially smart or successful, she always felt kind of uncomfortable around them. She never knew what to say to them because they were *really* smart and she knew she wasn't. Anything she had to say would come out sounding stupid. So she hardly said anything at all.

This wasn't very much fun, having to keep quiet all the time so as not to sound stupid.

So she knew she couldn't have an onion union with a really smart onion because she would never be good enough. But this nice male onion didn't make her feel that way. Even though he was a successful businessonion, she was more successful than he was. She was making more money than he was, which all onions know is the way to measure success in life.

So she decided that maybe she was good enough for *this* nice male onion and they should have an onion union. So they did.

All the onions in both their families and every onion they ever knew sent them wonderful presents and came to the ceremony to celebrate the union. All the onions who came to the ceremony were smiling and happy, and she knew she was supposed to be *especially* smiling and happy, so she smiled and smiled and tried to be happy, but what she was really feeling was *scared!*

She was *terrified*! Suddenly she realized that this union was a ridiculous idea. It would never work. All the things she had always known came flooding back to her. She could never belong. She could never be taken care of. This whole union idea was obviously *not going to work!*

And she felt another layer of onion skin growing under her union gown.

Since she had already agreed to this union idea and every onion in the *world* was there at the ceremony, she couldn't very well run away, so she just kept smiling and trying to look happy and not spoil the ceremony. This good front must have worked, because everyone said the union ceremony was beautiful, and none of the other onions could tell how scared she was.

After the ceremony and a trip to Bermuda called an "onionmoon," she came back home determined to do her best to be a good houseonion.

She knew deep inside that there was something different about her. She didn't quite understand it, but somehow she knew she wasn't meant to be a houseonion the way most girl onions were meant to be houseonions. And she knew this was going to be difficult for her, but she really *wanted* this union to work.

Then she had an idea. Being hard-working had made her appear to be smart, even though she wasn't really smart. So maybe if she worked hard enough, she could make herself appear to be a good houseonion. Maybe if she worked really, really hard, she could even make herself *be* a good houseonion. This was it! If she *worked hard enough* at it, she could *make it happen!* She could *make* this union work!

So she began to work very hard at this union. And it served her well. Her male onion thought she was a great houseonion. She did all the things a houseonion was supposed to do, and she found she even enjoyed some of them because they were such a nice change from being a businessonion and much less demanding. It was kind of like a vacation. She used to call it "playing houseonion" because it wasn't really her, but it was kind of fun.

And she felt her onion skin grow heavier and tighter, but she ignored it.

9

She and her male onion had many good years together. They even had a baby onion, who was all shiny and beautiful and was a joy and a pleasure to both of them.

But then, as so often happens, things began to change. As time went on, her onion skin began to feel tighter and tighter. It got very uncomfortable. And it began to hurt her. She tried to tell herself it wasn't that bad, but it just kept getting tighter. And it hurt even more. It really, really hurt. She didn't understand why, and she found herself blaming the male onion for hurting her. She knew he didn't want to hurt her, but she hurt whenever he was around, so it felt like he was hurting her.

She didn't want to feel the pain because she really wanted this union to work—especially now that they had a baby onion.

And all onions knew that if you split an onion union, it would "spoil" the baby onion.

She told herself she wasn't hurting. But of course she really was. Then she thought maybe if she could figure out where the pain was coming from, maybe she could make it stop. It was hard even to think clearly when she was hurting this badly, but she knew she had to figure this out because she couldn't go on like this forever.

She thought and thought. And hurt and hurt. And thought and thought. And hurt and hurt. Finally she just allowed herself to *feel* the pain instead of trying to pretend it wasn't there or it wasn't that bad. Once she allowed herself to feel it and look at it, she suddenly knew where it was coming from!

She had covered herself entirely with the skin of a houseonion, and it *just didn't fit!* The more she had struggled and tried to fix it, the tighter it got. And the more it hurt. All her hard work had made her *look* exactly like a houseonion. But she *wasn't* a houseonion, and the skin just *didn't fit!*

Of course it wasn't the male onion's fault. He was still the same nice onion she had married. He wasn't the one who was hurting her. It was the houseonion skin that was hurting her, and she had to get *out* of that skin!

But wait a minute! What about the baby onion! If you split an onion union, wouldn't that "spoil" the baby onion? She loved the baby onion so much that she would never do anything that might "spoil" the baby onion, no matter how much pain she was in herself.

So she told herself she could stand the pain if it would keep from "spoiling" the baby onion. So she stayed on and kept on wearing the houseonion skin, even though it kept hurting her more and more. She kept on wearing that houseonion skin, to keep from "spoiling" the baby onion she loved so much.

But she began to notice a strange and unexpected thing about the baby onion. Every time the mother onion or the father onion felt pain or did something that caused each other pain, the baby onion seemed to be in pain. In fact, once she began to really notice, the mother onion realized that the baby onion was "spoiling"!

Oh, no! This was the very thing she had been trying so hard to prevent! How could this happen? What should she do?

Now it was time for more thinking. Sensible onions had always said that splitting an onion union "spoils" the baby onions. But here she was, desperately trying to hold this union together, and her baby onion was "spoiling" before her very eyes. How could this be?

She gave a lot of thought to unions and splitting and what causes baby onions to "spoil." And she figured it out!

When onions split their unions, it's usually because one of the onions believes the other onion is totally "rotten." Sometimes both of them feel that way. And this causes pain. Each of them feels pain, and then they try to cause the other onion pain because each onion is convinced that the other onion is the cause of their own pain. And all of this pain between the parent onions causes the baby onion a *lot* of pain. And that "spoils" the baby onion.

That's it! It's *not splitting* that "spoils" baby onions! It's *pain* that "spoils" baby onions!

Now here we have a strange situation. We have a *union* that's causing pain, and that is "spoiling" the baby onion. But if we split this union and relieve the pain, the baby onion can be healthy and not "spoiled."

Neither of the parent onions is "rotten." They are both fine onions. It's just that for years, one of them has been wearing a skin that doesn't fit, and that's what has caused pain for all the onions.

Once she realized this, she gave a big tug at her tight, heavy houseonion skin. And it burst open and fell away from her.

The two parent onions split their union in a very peaceful and friendly way. They both agreed they were not meant to live in an onion union, but they would always work together to do whatever was best for their precious baby onion as she was growing up.

And they did this very well. The mother onion felt very relieved to be out of that tight houseonion skin, and the baby onion was not "spoiled." She was healthy and beautiful.

10

So it was time for the mother onion to get back to being a businessonion again and take care of herself and her baby. She was excited about doing this, but then an old feeling came back to her—a feeling that was very familiar from the past.

What if she wasn't good enough? What if she wasn't smart enough? She had spent a lot of years being a houseonion. What if she had forgotten everything she used to know as a businessonion? What if the things she used to know weren't good enough anymore?

Other onions told her she did know enough and she was smart enough, but she couldn't believe them. They were just being nice to make her feel better, but they couldn't be right. She had to do something to get smarter.

Then she had a great idea! She would go back to onion school and get some more letters attached to her! This was something she knew how to do. She was good at getting letters attached to her, and it had worked in the past. Other onions thought these letters made you smart.

So she did go to still another Onion University to get some more letters attached to her. (This time, the letters were "M.B.A.") By this time, she knew the letters wouldn't really *make* her smart, but they could make her *appear* smart, which she thought would be useful. And it was.

She did have to work very hard to get these letters attached, but she was good at working hard. And it served her well. Some businessonions (who should have known better) actually believed the letters meant she was smart, and she was offered a very good job. She went to work for a very important kind of onion business where it's their business to tell other businesses how to run their business. She found this kind of business very exciting, she worked hard at it, and she was successful.

She felt good. She felt good that her baby was not "spoiled," and she felt good that she was being successful again as a businessonion and making enough money to take care of herself and her baby.

But once again, as so often happens, things began to change. Some new onions bought the onion business she was working for, and they had a different way of running the business. They no longer wanted her to do the kind of work she enjoyed and was good at. They had their own ideas, and she tried her best to do what they wanted. She continued to work hard, but it was a struggle and she never felt she was doing it right. In fact, every day when she went to work, she felt pain. And she realized where the pain was coming from.

She had grown another layer of onion skin underneath her businessonion suit. And it was tight and heavy.

Now she had a real dilemma. This onion business was paying her a lot of money, which she needed to take care of herself and her baby. But it was also causing her a lot of pain. Maybe if she tried a different business, she could feel joy instead of pain. But a different business might not make as much money, and then she wouldn't be able to take care of her baby, and her baby would "spoil."

Maybe she should just put up with the pain so that her baby wouldn't be "spoiled."

No! Wait a minute! This was the same way she had felt when her onion union was causing her pain. And she had learned that *pain* will "spoil" a baby onion. Living in pain would not help her baby. She needed to do something to relieve the pain. She needed to find a different onion business.

She thought about this for a long time, and then she had a great idea! She had an idea for a business she thought other onions really needed. She would provide a service that would really help other onions. They would be willing to pay her good money for it. And it would give her joy and happiness to do this work. This would be great—to earn good money doing work you enjoy and believe in!

This idea made her feel so excited and so happy that she actually left the onion business that had been paying her a good, steady income and started her own onion business!

She was excited, but she was also scared. Starting an onion business is a risk. It might be hugely successful, and this made her feel excited. But it could fail completely, and this made her feel scared. Some onions told her she was crazy to give up a steady paycheck. And when they said this, she was afraid they were right. But then she would remember the pain she had felt every day at the old onion business, and she couldn't believe life was meant to be lived in this much pain.

She truly believed in her new idea. She knew it would bring her joy and happiness to do this work she believed in. And it certainly should be possible to be successful doing work you believe in.

11

By now, she knew what to do: Work hard. She made a plan for her new onion business, and she worked hard at it. Very, very hard. For what seemed like a very long time.

But things didn't go the way she had planned. It had been almost a year, and it looked like her new onion business wasn't working. It wasn't making money.

Lots of other onions told her she had a fine idea, and they said she had done a fine job of putting this new onion business together. But it wasn't making money. Maybe it never would make money.

This was awful! Her whole plan was falling apart! Nothing was working!

Her plan wasn't going to work. Nothing was going to work. She was spending her own money and she wasn't making any money and she wasn't going to make any money and all her money would be gone and she wouldn't be able to take care of herself and her baby!

What had she done! What had she done to herself and her baby! She had thought her plan was so good! And if it worked, it would bring joy and happiness to herself and her baby!

But it wasn't working! Maybe it wasn't going to work! Maybe she should never have tried this plan! Maybe she didn't have the right to seek joy and happiness! Maybe she should have just stuck with being hard-working! She had thought she was being brave to seek joy, but maybe she was just being foolish!

Maybe joy didn't exist! Or maybe she just didn't deserve it!

What had she done! What would become of her and her baby!

And she was scared! Really, really scared!

And her worst fear was that if she failed, it would "spoil" her baby.

12

She tried not to be scared because she knew being scared only made it harder to keep going. And she knew she had to hold herself together and keep going because her baby was depending on her. And she was afraid if she admitted to herself how scared she was, it would destroy her.

She thought back over the old ways that had worked for her before. And she decided she must not be working hard enough. Because hard-working had always been the answer before. So if she wasn't getting where she needed to be, it must mean she wasn't working hard enough.

She thought that must be right, but somehow it just didn't *feel* right. She knew she was already working hard, but she felt like there was something blocking her. Like she kept pushing and pushing, but there was a wall there and she couldn't break through.

She felt there was a "right path" for her, and she knew there were obstacles on every path. She *thought* she was on her "right path," so it must be that she just needed to keep pushing until she got through the obstacles. So she kept pushing and kept working hard.

And as she was working hard, she also read lots of onion books, hoping that one of them would give her the answer she was looking for. In one of these onion books, she read something that for some reason caught her attention. It said, *"When the student is ready, the teacher will appear."*

Maybe there was something else to learn. Something other than what she had always been doing. Maybe there was another teacher out there. If so, she was ready to learn.

13

One day, when she was at one of her regular meetings of businessonions, she happened to sit next to two other businessonions who were talking about some sort of "process."

This was a process they had been through themselves. And they knew others who had been through the process. They said this process had actually changed their lives. It had really helped them to get what they want—not only in their onion business, but in being with other onions and in doing whatever it was they really wanted to do.

These businessonions got very excited as they talked about this process. In fact, she thought they actually looked kind of sparkly and shiny whenever they talked about this process.

She didn't know exactly what this process was or how it worked, and they said it was very difficult to explain. But she didn't care. It seemed to have made them sparkly and shiny and enabled them to do what they wanted to do. If it could make her sparkly and shiny and enable her to do what she wanted to do, then whatever this process was, she wanted it!

So she asked them what to do in order to get this process for herself, and they told her she had to make a *commitment* to it. She wasn't so sure about making a commitment to something she didn't fully understand. Especially when there was, after all, no guarantee that this process would actually work for *her*.

So she thought about it for a while, and she talked to still others who had been through the process. And they, too, seemed all sparkly and shiny whenever they talked about the process. In fact, there was something about these others that made her feel just a little bit sparkly and shiny herself when she was with them.

So what was stopping her? Why didn't she just make a commitment to do this process?

It was fear! Fear that it wouldn't turn out right, fear that she was making a mistake, fear that others would think her foolish.

Suddenly she realized something. She had those same fears about her business—and her life! Fear that it wouldn't turn out, fear of what others were thinking, fear that she wasn't good enough. It was fear that haunted her and made her feel stopped in what she was trying to do in life.

She wanted to do this process, and for once she wasn't going to let fear stop her. Maybe this process could even help her handle her fears.

So even though she was still a little afraid of what it was and how it would turn out, she chose to have faith in this process, and she made a commitment to it.

It was a funny thing that happened then. Once she made the commitment to this process, she started to feel better, even though the process itself hadn't actually started yet. She felt like she had taken the first step in getting past her fears. Maybe fear was the wall she had been pushing up against. Maybe that's what had been blocking her. Maybe this process was actually going to get her through that wall.

She didn't really understand how the process could have started working already. Did it have something to do with the commitment? Or was it recognizing her fear and stepping past it? She didn't know. And she found she didn't much care. If it was already starting to help her, what difference did it make?

14

Finally it was time for the process itself to start, and she was really excited about it. She went to the place where they told her to go, to do the process. It wasn't any kind of a special place—just a place. A place where she could get away from the regular onion world and do the process.

There were all kinds of other onions there who had also made a commitment to do the process. They seemed like nice onions, but she was a little worried. They didn't look very shiny or sparkly—just eager, and a little bit worried themselves.

There was a leader who was there to help all the onions with the process, and she wasn't quite sure how she felt about this leader and whether this process was really going to work. But he seemed sparkly and shiny, and she decided to trust him. The leader said some things for all the onions to think about, but she wasn't sure they applied to her, and this made her uncomfortable. How was this going to work? This process wasn't so great. How could it possibly help her?

But she kept saying to herself, "Remember your commitment, and just turn yourself over to the process. Don't resist it. Give it a chance to work."

This helped her to get past the worrying and to really listen to what the leader was saying. At one point, she thought she heard him saying something very strange. The leader was suggesting, of all things, that maybe their onion skins were too tight! And he would help to loosen them!

She thought this very peculiar. But she remembered she had come here to have the process help her, and in order for this to work, she had to *let* it help her. In fact, she had to *help* it help her. So she decided to try her best to help it help her, by doing whatever the leader suggested, no matter how peculiar.

And so she did.

As the process went on, she realized that it was actually like a conversation. But this conversation was very different from any she had ever had before. In this conversation, all the onions were being *totally honest*—really sharing their lives and their feelings with each other.

She had never been in a conversation that was so honest before. In most conversations, all the onions are just polishing up their own onion skins, saying whatever they think will make them look good to other onions.

But these onions weren't polishing their own skins at all. She could see that it was sometimes very difficult for these other onions to be so honest. Sometimes they shared things that were very painful—experiences or feelings they had kept hidden for a long time. She knew they were afraid of sharing these things—afraid they would look dull, brown, or ugly, afraid the other onions would reject them once they knew the truth.

But there was something about this process that made these onions feel safe to tell the truth about their own lives. And something very strange always happened. Whenever these onions shared something very difficult, it didn't make them look dull, brown, or ugly. In fact, they always looked rather shiny and sparkly after sharing themselves. And the other onions didn't reject them. In fact, just the opposite occurred. Whenever these onions shared something difficult—fear, pain, struggle, weakness—other onions embraced them and thanked them. In fact, sometimes other onions would say, "Thank you for sharing that. You spoke for me."

She found this amazing and very disturbing. Here she had devoted all her efforts for all these years to building up her own layers of onion skin and polishing them constantly so she would look good to other onions. Wasn't this what you were supposed to do in order to be successful, to be accepted, to belong?

It was a lot of effort, constantly polishing her onion skin in order to look good. Could it be possible that this wasn't necessary? Maybe it doesn't even work? Maybe other onions don't even notice my skin, they're so busy polishing their own? What is it that's so appealing when we stop polishing and reveal what's under the onion skin?

She didn't understand what was happening, but she decided to try sharing something of herself. She shared about how she had always wanted to belong but never did fit in. She even shared about wanting to be a "cheeronion" because that would make her little, cute, and pretty. And she shared about how clumsy, awkward, and ugly she had always felt.

All the time she was sharing these things, it made her cry because she was so embarrassed to reveal her deepest fears. She was convinced that once the other onions realized how clumsy and awkward and insecure she was, they would want nothing to do with her. They would know she was not good enough to belong, she just didn't fit in.

Much to her amazement, the other onions *loved* the things she shared. They thanked her for having the courage to speak the truth. Many of them said she spoke for them, and it made them feel better about themselves. They hugged her and said they felt very close to her. They even said she sparkled while she was sharing.

This was an incredible experience. Could this possibly be true? What makes others feel close to me and want to be with me is not the good front I've devoted my life to keeping up. It's not how well I polish my onion skin. It's when I give up the good front and reveal the truth that's inside. Maybe I could quit polishing this onion skin. Maybe there's something better underneath it.

She wasn't sure, but she thought she felt her onion skin get looser.

15

For a while, she just watched the other onions and listened to what they had to say. She noticed that some were not speaking at all, but they seemed to be very moved by what the others were sharing.

She found that being in a conversation with so many onions being so honest about their own lives gave her a profound understanding she had never had before. She began to realize she was not alone. The issues she struggled with were not unique to her. They were part of the *design* of being an onion.

She had spent her life up to this point convinced she was the only onion who always felt not good enough. She was also convinced that this was *the truth*—she really *wasn't good enough.* She worked very hard to *appear* smart, capable, and self-confident. But she was always afraid the other onions would find out she wasn't really smart, or capable, or confident. It was just an act, a good front she kept up so no one would know how inadequate she really was.

She had always thought she could tell just by looking at other onions that they really *were* smart, capable, and self-confident. They really *knew* what they were doing and never felt insecure like she did. She could never let them know what she was feeling inside because they didn't feel insecure. She had to keep up the good front so she could be like them.

But here, in this conversation, in this process, she suddenly realized that all the other onions were exactly like her! Every one of them had the same kind of experience that she did—feeling not good enough the way they were. Every one of them thought they should be different from how they were. They should be better-looking, smarter, taller, shorter, heavier, thinner, whatever. And every one of them put on a good front so no one else would know how inadequate they felt.

What a concept! No one is really what they appear to be. We all feel not good enough, but we keep polishing these layers of onion skin so no one will find out how we really feel. What if feeling not good enough is just part of the way onions are designed? What if it's not "the truth"? What if this feeling doesn't mean anything about who we actually are and what we are capable of? Maybe I can just acknowledge this feeling as part of being an onion, but not let it run my life.

This time, she was sure she felt her onion skin get looser.

16

She was feeling pretty relaxed and pretty good about how this process was going when, without any warning at all, the leader said something that made her stomach queasy and her hands sweaty. He started talking about fear.

Fear! The thing that haunted her, that paralyzed her whenever she thought about what she was trying to do and how she might fail. The very thought of this fear made it hard for her to concentrate on what the leader was saying. But he was asking them not to fight their fears, not to push them away, but to let them in, to experience them, to just *be* with their feelings and their fears.

At first she tried not to think about what was deep inside her because she knew if she did, she would cry. And she didn't want to cry. Because she was afraid if she let down her guard, she would fall apart. But these feelings were causing her pain, and they were getting stronger and stronger.

Finally the feelings inside her were so strong she couldn't keep fighting them anymore, so she just allowed herself to *feel* them. And as she allowed herself to feel them and to recognize them, she started to cry. And she found that as she cried, she felt better because the crying was letting the feelings out. So she didn't try to stop herself anymore. She just cried and cried and let all the feelings come out.

I feel alone. I know I'm not really alone, but it feels that way. What am I doing? What have I done? I'm supposed to take care of myself and my baby. I've said I would, and I have to because nobody else will. Or maybe they would, but it wouldn't be right to ask them. I have to do it myself.

But what have I done? I feel like I've jumped off a cliff into space without knowing at all what's out there. It's one thing to take a risk for myself, to try to seek happiness and joy, but what about my baby? Do I have the right to do this to my baby? What if I can't do it? What if I'm not good enough? What if I'm going to crash at the bottom of this cliff, and I've dragged my baby down with me? What have I done? What will become of us? *I'm afraid!*

And she cried and cried because she felt alone and she was afraid for herself and her baby. Until finally, there was nothing left to cry about anymore. All the feelings and all the fear had been let out. She felt a great sense of relief, once all the fear had been let out, and there was an empty space were the fear had been.

She remembered the leader had said to ask for what she needed and the universe would answer her. So she asked for the strength and the wisdom and the courage to take care of herself and her baby, because she was afraid for them and felt alone and felt she wasn't good enough.

And the universe did answer her, and it was the Caretaker. He told her she was not alone. He was with her, and He believed in her. He told her that she *was* good enough and always had been. She should not fear for her baby because He would help her take care of her baby. And He told her He wanted her to be "unreasonably happy," that He wanted her to feel "irrational joy."

And the space where the fear had been was filled up with faith. Faith that the universe would support her, that it was right for her to seek happiness and joy, that she would be able to take care of herself and her baby, that she was good enough, and she was not alone.

She felt a huge sense of relief, and for some reason she felt much lighter. Like something really heavy had been stripped off her.

All of a sudden, she realized what she was feeling. It felt like her onion skin had come loose and was being stripped away. Then she looked down and saw that in fact two big, heavy layers of onion skin had fallen off and were lying at her feet.

This is strange! It feels good, but it feels strange! It's like I'm peeling off these layers of onion skin to get to something inside.

I wonder what's inside. What could be inside? And then she got it!

What's inside is a diamond!

A diamond! Of all things, a diamond!

I'm really not an onion after all!

I am a diamond!

A DIAMOND WEARING AN ONION SUIT!!

17

She found this hilarious! She found she couldn't help laughing! She laughed and laughed and couldn't stop laughing!

This is ridiculous! I am ridiculous! I'm a diamond wearing an onion suit! How ridiculous! Diamonds are beautiful! Onions are silly! If I'm really a diamond, why would I want to wear an onion suit!

Wait! I just realized something else! We're all diamonds! We're all diamonds wearing onion suits! We only think we're onions because we're all wearing onion suits! We think we need this skin to protect us, but it makes us all think we're onions! No wonder life is such a struggle! We all keep struggling and struggling to be good onions, but that's impossible because we're really diamonds!

But diamonds are better than onions! Diamonds are something! Onions are nothing!

Why would a diamond want to wear an onion suit! I'm taking off this stupid onion suit!

She gave a little tug, and a big layer of onion skin fell off. And she felt better. Much better.

She sat there for a while, just enjoying this feeling.

18

Then, suddenly she made another discovery. She figured out where her onion suit had come from!

Her parents had put one on her when she was little. She had been shiny and sparkly then, but her parents were afraid that if she sparkled too much, the ones in the onion suits would hurt her because she didn't look like them. Her parents knew that other onions don't like it if you sparkle a lot because you're very smart. So they had put a little onion suit on her, just to protect her.

And it did. But because she was wearing it, she didn't know she was a diamond. She thought she was an onion. And she thought that whenever she felt afraid, the thing to do was to put on another layer of onion skin to protect her.

But the more she tried to protect herself, the more she was hiding her diamondness! Every layer of onion skin she put on took her further and further away from her diamondness.

These onion suits are a sham! They're a fake! They're a trap! You only think they're protecting you, but what they're really doing is *hiding* you! Hiding your real self and your diamondness from the world because you're afraid!

These onion suits are uncomfortable! And they're heavy! And they don't fit! And they don't work!

I'm taking this stupid onion suit off!

So she gave a harder tug, and this time several big layers of onion skin fell off. And she felt better. Much, much better.

19

Then she gave a lot of thought as to how she had come to be wearing such a big, heavy onion suit. Maybe her parents had put the first little layers on her just to protect her, but she had been adding more and more layers *herself* all the rest of her life. How had she done this?

She thought about this for a long time, until she finally got it! Every time something happened in her life, she would attach a certain meaning to it. They were usually meanings like . . .

They don't like me.
I'm not good enough.
I don't fit in.
I don't really belong.

It had never occurred to her that whatever meaning she made up wasn't "the truth." She had thought she knew what it really meant when something happened—the only meaning.

But it wasn't! Whatever she made up wasn't the only possible meaning. There were lots of other possible meanings to anything that happened. Maybe we could never know the real meaning of things. Maybe there is no *real* meaning—only different interpretations that people make up.

Wasn't it silly that she always made up meanings that felt heavy and uncomfortable!

All these old meanings were just her onion suit! And she had put it on herself! But, if she could put it on herself, she could take it off herself. If she was the one who had created the old meanings, then she had the power to create *new* meanings. Better meanings. Ones that *did work* for her. Meanings that made her feel good about herself, that allowed her to sparkle.

She thought back to the times when she had put on some of these layers. When she first started onion school and was moved from the 1B to the 1A, she had made that mean she didn't fit in. Maybe it meant she was smart because she already knew how to read. She remembered junior onion school when she wasn't little, cute, and pretty and had made that mean she could never belong. Maybe it only meant she was like the little duckling who just needed to be patient until she grew into a graceful swan.

Each time she gave up one of these old meanings, another layer of onion skin fell off and lay at her feet.

This onion suit is stupid! I don't need it! I don't want it! I'm taking it off! All off!

She gave a *big* tug, and all the rest of the layers fell off. And she felt *very sparkly!*

Then she heard the universe speak to her again, and it was the voice of the Caretaker. And He said to her, "I've got great plans for you. Your life is going to be *just great!* You're going to *love* your life—and live it powerfully!

And she believed it. She knew it was true. She knew there was a "right path" for her. She didn't know if it was the path she was already on, or an entirely different path. But she knew it would come to her if she would just trust and let it happen.

Whatever was right for her, she would know it. She would feel it. She would do it. And so she trusted. And she felt peace. And she felt great!

This was amazing! She felt like she had been transformed. She still had concerns about how things would turn out, but fear no longer overwhelmed her. She knew she had to keep working to do her part, but she now completely trusted that the universe and the Caretaker would support her and her baby.

When she tried to think logically about all this, she found it very strange that she felt so much better, so much calmer, so optimistic, and so empowered. Her circumstances had not changed during this process she had just been through. What had changed was the way she viewed them, the way she felt about them, and the confidence she felt in her ability to deal with them.

Was this the power of faith? The power of commitment? The power of this process? Or the power that had always been inside her that had been covered up? The power of living life as a diamond?

20

Wait a minute! If everybody has the power to live life as a diamond, why doesn't everybody take off their onion suits?

And the answer came to her. To be able to take off your onion suit, *you have to believe in diamonds!* And it's hard to believe in diamonds when the world appears to be filled with onions.

After thinking this over, she realized that if she was brave enough and strong enough to just *be* a diamond and let her light shine on others, that would help them to believe in diamonds. Maybe they could even believe there was a diamond hidden under their own onion suit. And when they saw how great life was for her as a diamond, maybe that would help them have the courage to take off their own onion suits.

Then she had a thought that scared her. Since most of us have never actually seen a diamond and have only seen onions, if she went running around as a diamond, everyone would think she was just a really weird, funny-looking onion! And they would think she wasn't good enough! And she wouldn't fit in! And she could never belong! Then she got really, really scared!

What was happening here? She couldn't figure out why she felt so scared when she had felt so good just a few minutes ago. Then she looked down and realized she was wearing her onion suit again!

Without even thinking about what she was doing, she had put her onion suit back on again the minute she started to feel scared! But the onion suit wasn't working!

It had never worked! Throughout her life, every time she had felt scared, she had just added more layers. But it hadn't ever worked! It had just gotten heavier and hotter. She had thought it was protecting her, but it wasn't! It never had! It was a joke! A fraud! A sham! A costume!

It didn't protect her! It only made her look like an onion! How ridiculous! A diamond wearing an onion suit! How stupid!

How silly I am, covering a beautiful diamond with an onion suit. How silly we all are. How silly life is. What a relief!

And the onion suit fell off.

21

She thought about all this for a very long time.

She thought about how really great life would be for everybody if they could all find the courage to take off their onion suits.

She knew she was willing to be a diamond for all the world to see, but she wondered if maybe there was something more she could do.

This whole thing about being a diamond was so new to her. She wasn't sure just what she could do to help others be diamonds. Or if she could really make a difference.

Then she remembered the process and how they had talked about the power of your word, the power of commitment. "I am what I say I am. If I say it, I can make it so. I can create myself. I can create my future. I am what I say I am."

For the first time, she really understood her own power. She felt strong. She felt good.

And she knew what she could do to help. She sat down and started to write.

www.ingramcontent.com/pod-product-compliance
Lightning Source LLC
Chambersburg PA
CBHW071201130626
46555CB00004B/1541